For all the young Joneses, Hodgsons, Holdens and Slowiks with love – J.J.

For Freddy – A.C.

With special thanks to Meridian Art London who represent Jenny Jones

First published in 1999 by Macmillan Children's Books.
This edition published 2000 for The Book People Ltd,
Hall Wood Avenue, Haydock, St Helens, WA11 9UL.

ISBN 0 333 73594 3 (HB)
ISBN 0 333 73595 1 (PB)

1 3 5 7 9 8 6 4 2

A CIP catalogue record for this book is available
from the British Library

Printed in Belgium

Danny
and the
Great White
Bear

Written by Anne Cottringer

Illustrated by Jenny Jones

TED SMART

Danny and his dad looked
up at the night sky. The stars
glinted above their heads, but
Danny felt sad. His dad was
going far away the
next day.

"See that cluster of stars up there?" said his dad. "It's called the Great Bear." Danny had to look hard to see the bear, but he could just make one out. "Before you go to sleep, look up at those stars. Wherever I am, I'll look up at them, too, and I'll be thinking of you."

The next morning Danny and his mum waved goodbye to his dad. Dad often went away to take pictures of wild animals. Danny loved the pictures, but he never got used to the goodbyes.

He tried not to be sad. He tried not to be cross.
He tried to be a big boy.

He was just about to chew his thumb, when there
was a knock at the door. Before Danny could get up
to answer it . . .

. . . a great white bear strolled in.

He looked around, poked his head in and out of cupboards, tested the bounce on Danny's bed and decided to stay. Danny called him White Bear.

White Bear travelled lightly. In a bag with a strap he had paper and pens and some frozen fish fingers which he put in the fridge, in case he got hungry.

At first Danny didn't tell his mum
about the bear, but it's hard to keep
a big white bear a secret in a small house.
    "He can stay as long as he behaves,"
said his mum.

In the morning
White Bear took
Danny to school.

He held Danny's
hand all the way there.

He waved until Danny
had disappeared
through the school
doors.

After school they went swimming. They dipped and dived and sprayed and splashed. When he was tired, Danny flopped across White Bear's big, wet belly.

At night, before bed, Danny and White Bear read stories together.

And after his mum had kissed him goodnight, and the dark was close, Danny slipped out of bed and looked up at the night sky. The Great Bear was still there.

For days and weeks, White
Bear stayed with Danny.
He scared away the
neighbour's dog.

He helped Danny
build his train set.

He pushed Danny on the
swing in the park.

And when Danny fell, he
put a plaster on his knee.

Occasionally, when White Bear
got hungry, Danny's mum cooked
some fish fingers.

Then one day a postcard came from Danny's
dad. The picture showed a land of ice and
snow and an enormous starry sky.
　"White Bear! Look!" cried Danny.
"Look where my dad is!" On the back of
the postcard was a message:

> *Dear Danny,*
> *home soon!*
> *love, Dad.*

White Bear looked a bit sad.
　"Are you missing home?"
asked Danny. White Bear
chewed on his big paw.

Danny fetched White Bear's pens. He spread out a snowy white sheet of paper and helped White Bear write a letter:

Dear Folks,
home soon!
love, White Bear.

They posted it the next day on the way to school.

That evening Danny and White Bear looked up at the Great Bear and then, in the starry darkness, they climbed into bed.

Danny couldn't sleep. The quiet was too quiet. The night was too long. He wondered where his dad was now. Beside him, White Bear lay awake, too.

Finally Danny went to sleep. White Bear gathered up his paper and pens, strapped his bag on his back and slipped silently down the stairs.

Light was just beginning to seep in at the edge
of the sky when Danny woke up.
    White Bear was gone!

Danny was just about to chew his thumb when
he heard a key in the front door . . .
footsteps on the stairs . . .
his door opened a crack.

"Dad!" cried Danny, leaping out of bed and into his father's arms.

"Did you look at the Great Bear every night?" asked his dad.

"I did!" said Danny. "And a Great White Bear came to stay while you were away."

"I hope you looked after each other," said his dad.

Danny looked up at the Great Bear in the sky.
"I'll save the rest of the fish fingers for next
time!" he whispered to the stars.
And the stars winked back at him.